W9-BQY-222

The Golden Bird

The Golden Bird

HANS STOLP

Illustrations by
Lidia Postma

Dial Books for Young Readers
New York

First published in the United States 1990 by
Dial Books for Young Readers
A Division of Penguin Books USA Inc.
2 Park Avenue
New York, New York 10016

Published in the Netherlands 1987 by Lemniscaat Publishers
as *De Gouden Vogel: dagboek van een stervende jongen*

Design by Judith M. Lanfredi

Printed in the U.S.A.
First Edition
E
10 9 8 7 6 5 4 3 2 1

Library of Congress Cataloging in Publication Data
Stolp, Hans. The golden bird.
Translation of: De gouden vogel dagboek
van een stervende jongen.
Summary: Engaged in a losing battle with cancer,
eleven-year-old Daniel is comforted by many people but finds
his greatest solace in the vision of a phoenix-like golden
bird and its vision of promise and renewal.
[1. Cancer—Fiction. 2. Death—Fiction]
I. Postma, Lidia, ill. II. Title.
PZ7.S875835Go 1990 [Fic] 89-11893
ISBN 0-8037-0681-2 ISBN 0-8037-0751-7 (lib. bdg.)

The Golden Bird

My stomach hurts. I wish it would stop. I don't like it. It feels a little better when I lie on my back, but it's boring lying on your back all the time. I try turning on my side, but not for long—I turn on my back again a minute later.

Soon they'll give me more medicine. I used to pull the sheet over my head when the nurse came with medicine. Now I look forward to it.

Where's Mom? I wish she was here. She doesn't have to talk, just be here beside me.

I see three birds on the windowsill outside: a golden one, a blue one, and a green one. The golden bird's in the middle, with the blue bird on the left and the green bird on the right. The golden bird is pecking at its feathers. Do birds itch too?

The blue bird turns its head a little to one side and looks at me out of one eye. Its eye is dark, with a gold rim around it. I think the blue bird is beautiful. It looks so serious, though. When I smile, it nods its head at me, the way pigeons do, and ruffles its feathers. The feathers have a blue glow.

The blue bird startles me by opening its beak and speaking out loud, saying, "My name's Victor." I hear him quite clearly. Victor—I like that name. He walks along the windowsill, then gives me another serious glance before he spreads his wings and flies away.

The green bird follows. There are flashes of yellow in its outstretched green wings, like those in peacock feathers. I watch them get smaller and smaller until they're only specks in the distant sky. Finally they vanish.

The golden bird has stopped preening its feathers. Its eyes are blue, pale blue, as pale as the water in the sea. I feel myself being drawn toward its eyes. I float up from my bed and feel happy. Then suddenly the golden bird flies away too, and I'm back in my bed. My stomach hurts again and yet I still feel happy inside.

Mom smiled when I told her about the birds. "What a lovely dream," she told me. It wasn't a dream, though. I really did see them. Maybe they'll come back tomorrow.

I dreamed about Dad last night. He's been dead for a long time—about four years, I think. That's right, I was seven when it happened. I remember that morning really well. I'd gotten up early, when it was just turning light outside. I went downstairs to the living room and took a big book off the shelf and looked at the pictures. I enjoyed doing that. It was very quiet. The paperboy rode by on his bike, whistling, and I heard some birds singing—nothing else. Then I heard steps from upstairs. Dad came down in his pajamas, which was strange because he was usually the last one up. His pajamas had red and white stripes.

"Up already?" he asked me. "I'm going to make some tea. Would you like a little, with lots of milk? I'm feeling kind of strange this morning."

He went into the kitchen, then I heard him put the teapot on the counter. He came back in and sat down in the big armchair, but he didn't say anything. Soon he began snoring, and his snores were slow and deep. I looked up. He was sitting strangely, his head thrown way back. He sighed deeply three times and then stopped. That was all.

I can't remember exactly what happened after that. I only know that Mom cried and cried, and I still hear that sound sometimes in my dreams.

Last night I dreamed that Dad was walking across a green field toward me. He wore a white suit and a blue shirt and he looked wonderful. He gave me a warm, happy smile. I wanted to run to him, but he put his hand up, calling out: "Not yet, Daniel! Soon . . . soon . . . and then I'll make us both some tea."

As far as I can remember, the dream ended there. Mom says that Daddy's in heaven. I wonder if they all wear light clothes there.

The I.V.—the thin intravenous tube that puts medicine directly into my blood system—has been taken out again. After a few days my left arm started to hurt and swell up in the place where the needle went in, so now it has to be moved to my foot. It hurts there more than in your arm. Helen, the nurse, will be here soon. I hope she'll find the best spot to put in the I.V. right away. Usually bags of liquid medicine are hanging from the I.V. stand, but now they're off, and I can see that the stand looks like a kind of cross. It's strange that I never noticed that before.

I wish that Mom was here. It's not so bad then, even though I yell louder when she's around. Maybe that's why they're putting the new I.V. in while she's away from my room: it's the fourth time they've done that.

Helen's okay. She says, "This will hurt, Daniel, but not for long." I used to have a nurse who said, "It'll be over in a second, and you'll hardly feel a thing." That's not true. It hurts when they put the I.V. in.

Helen comes in now, smiling at me. She knows

that it's hard, but she says that maybe it's best to just get it over with—though all of a sudden I just wish she'd go away and not come back all day. That feels mean, but it's hard not to feel mean sometimes.

I waited for Victor and the other birds all day, but they didn't come.

They measured my stomach again today; they do that twice a week. It's an inch bigger than it was last time.

Josh came this afternoon. He's thirteen. We used to share a room here, but now I'm on my own. Josh has cancer too, or really, he's *had* cancer—the course of treatment worked and now he only needs to come back for checkups. All his hair has grown back already, so you can't see that he ever lost hair during the treatments. He always comes to see me when he's in for checkups, either by himself or with his mother. He came in alone today. I noticed that he seemed shocked to see me—my stomach has gotten really big. Josh didn't stay long. I didn't know what to say, and neither did he.

I think Mom's got to lose some weight. She doesn't get enough exercise, sitting by my bed all day long. When I first told her that, she thought I was joking, but now she's promised to cut back on sugar and to eat less at lunch. Today she tried some tea without sugar for the first time and made a face over it. I'll have to keep an eye on her.

Victor's on the windowsill, alone. I didn't see him come. His feathers are glowing so strongly that it's as if a blue light is burning there. He gives me a little bow with his head, which makes me smile like last time. Suddenly he flies toward me through the window—right through the glass—yet the glass doesn't shatter, it stays intact as if nothing happened. He lands by my feet at the end of the bed. He looks beautiful.

"I've got something to tell you," he says. "The golden bird is building a nest near the sun, and when the nest is ready it will lay golden eggs in it which will hatch in the strong heat. The golden bird will come for you when all the chicks are born." Victor looks very solemn, but I feel happy. I wouldn't mind going soon.

"Will it take much longer?"

"Not much longer now," Victor says. He nods his head again and walks with his orange feet along the rail at the end of my bed. He ruffles his feathers and seems to hide his head in them in embarrassment. Then the feathers drop smoothly into place. "I'm going now," he says, "but I'll be back to see you every day, until the golden bird comes."

I watch him flutter his wings in the air and fly back out the window without breaking it. He gets smaller and smaller as he flies off into the blue sky. I watch him for so long that I don't even notice when Helen comes in. I jump when she puts her arm around me.

"Did you have a good nap?" she asks.

"I'll be flying to the golden bird's nest soon," I tell her.

Helen strokes my hair and says, "What wonderful dreams you have, Daniel." Why do grown-ups always think you've been dreaming when there's something they can't understand?

I wake up because I hear Mom crying, even though she's not in the room. But I recognize the sound of her sobbing, and it makes me feel cold inside. I'm afraid. Why is she crying? Has she spoken to the doctor again? She was going to. Maybe she saw him this afternoon.

I look around the room: at the television set on a stand against the wall opposite my bed, at the picture of Donald Duck that used to be my favorite when I was little. It's taped next to the television. He looks sad. In all the five months I've been here, it's the first time I've ever thought that.

I look outside. The sky is a sunny blue. I see a bird—a seagull, I think—disappear behind the window, slowly flapping its wings. The window's empty now except for blue sky. I wish that Victor was here, but he isn't. Is he helping the golden bird build the nest? I remember a picture in a book at school of a bird with straw in its beak, flying to its nest. Is Victor somewhere far away, with golden straw in his beak?

The room is the same as it always was. The television set, the picture, the cards on the wall, the empty bed next to mine, the I.V. Yet it looks different, too, as if things are farther away than usual, as if there's a kind of gray mist hanging over everything.

I can't hear the sound of Mom's crying anymore. It gradually stopped, becoming muffled by the sounds coming from the corridor and the lounge: of children's voices, of footsteps, of phones ringing.

My whole stomach's sore. If I lie still and breathe in very gently, it feels a little better.

The room's starting to look strange. Everything is slowly moving away from me. The wall with the television and Donald Duck is moving farther and farther back; Donald's blue coat is now a dot in the distance. The window's getting smaller all the time and going farther away. There's a big space growing between me and the empty bed beside me, and the door to the corridor seems a mile away. I'm all alone in a room that's bigger than any I've ever seen. There isn't any noise. It reminds me of a huge cathedral I visited once with Mom. It was just as big and quiet there, and on the side wall was a large cross with Jesus's body on it, the eyes half closed. I can still see that face. I remember how Mom pulled me away because I kept looking at it.

Mom has promised that when I'm better, we'll go all the way to New Zealand to see Aunt Beth. I've never met her. She lives on a farm and one of her children is named Daniel, like me. We were both named after Granddad. Daniel's six months older than I am. I close my eyes, and now the room doesn't seem so big and quiet. Victor will come tomorrow. I wonder what he'll say to me then.

When I wake up, I hear a quiet clicking sound in the room. I keep my eyes closed and listen to it: it's Mom, knitting by the side of my bed. The clicking stops and I open my eyes.

"Did you sleep well?"

"Yes."

Mom looks at me searchingly. I can tell from her eyes that she's been crying.

"Why did you cry?" I ask.

She picks up the sleeve of a blue sweater she's making and starts knitting again.

"Oh, I was feeling sad because it's hard for you

to be so sick and there's nothing I can do about it. You've been here so long." She knits very quickly.

"Have you talked to the doctor?"

"For a few minutes. He said that the tumor is still there. I asked if there are other treatments, or stronger ones. He told me he'd talk again to the other doctors." She doesn't look up. Her voice sounds funny, maybe from her crying.

I close my eyes. I feel cold inside again. I think of Victor and imagine him flying in the air. How wonderful to be so free.

I can't sleep. It must be about one o'clock in the morning. I wish it was light again. My mouth's dry and I'm sore. Everything's churning around inside me. I want to shout very loud, I don't know why. I don't shout, though. I hear small sounds but then realize that I'm making them myself, though I don't hear them until they're out.

I keep drifting off to the sound of voices, Mom's and the doctor's. In between, I hear her crying. It's strange, not being able to make out what they're saying.

I was asleep when the doctor came this afternoon, Mom told me. He usually comes to see me late in the afternoon and he doesn't say much, but normally I can tell from his expression whether he's pleased or not. The other day he frowned when he looked at my chart, and two deep wrinkles shot straight up from his eyebrows.

I wish I was home in my own bed. Being sick wouldn't be so bad then, I think. It's so confined here, with the I.V. stuff, then getting washed and weighed, having my stomach measured, and all the new things they keep thinking up to do. The cancer treatment, chemotherapy, is the worst. I don't really want to think about it, it only makes me feel sick.

After a long time I buzz for the nurse and tell her that I can't sleep. "Are you lying awake worrying?" she asks. I'm not worrying. It's just that I can't sleep. She says that if I'm not asleep soon, she'll bring me some sleeping medicine. "That'll help you get some rest," she says gently. She's new, and I haven't seen her before. Her name is Winnie. She looks nice.

Later the door opens quietly. The light streams in from the corridor and Winnie tiptoes over to me. She stands by my bed silently. We can just see each other in the darkness.

"Why are you crying, Danny?" she asks me softly.

"I'm not crying."

When she gently touches my face, I burst out in tears. Winnie holds me while I cry. I can't even

hear what it is I'm shouting, except the words "I'm scared!" over and over again.

Winnie goes on holding me after I've calmed down. I snuggle in closer to her. She doesn't talk and I'm glad. Finally she says, "I'll go find the medicine for you. Then maybe you'll be able to get some sleep."

I can see a blue dot outside in the distance, moving straight toward the window. It's Victor. I recognize him even before I can see him well. He flies awfully fast, and before I know it, he's down at the end of my bed again.

He grooms his feathers with his beak and nods his head at me, and I laugh. I can't help it.

"That's better, Daniel," he says. "I'm glad you can still laugh after last night."

"How do you know about last night?"

"The golden bird sees everything and knows everything. The golden bird told me about you this morning."

I listen in surprise. Somehow I know that it's true. I suddenly have an image of the golden bird, perched on the half-finished nest, with Victor on the ground below. I can hear the golden bird saying, "Tell Daniel not to be afraid."

"Why shouldn't I be afraid?" I ask.

Now it's Victor's turn to be startled. He looks at me and asks, "How did you know what I was going to say?"

Before I can answer, he shakes his head thoughtfully. "The golden bird told me, 'Remember, Daniel is a special person who knows more than he thinks he does.' " After a pause, Victor goes on: "The golden bird says that you should watch the tree outside your window. You may not have noticed it much before. Its branches are bare, and it may look dead to you, just the way it has looked all winter. But now, if you look more closely, you'll see buds on it. In a while the buds will start to bloom, until the whole tree will be covered in beautiful blossoms. It's a flowering cherry tree.

"So look carefully at the tree, and you'll see the buds forming. These will open into blossoms later. For you, too, there has been a kind of winter inside. But soon there will be a transformation, like the change from winter to spring. The transformation can be hard, Daniel, and it can even be painful. But don't be frightened, since it's really the time of blossoming that is coming closer. Once the blossoms come, the pain will be gone forever."

Victor stops, then says to me, "The golden bird says that if you get frightened again, you should think about the flowering cherry tree."

He flies to my bedstand, lands carefully on my pile of books, and pushes his beak into the glass of water to take a drink.

"Long stories like that make me thirsty," he says between gulps. After each gulp he throws back his head till his beak sticks up in the air, so that the water can slide down more easily. When he has finished, he looks at me and nods again.

"Don't forget, will you, Daniel? I was so worried about forgetting the story that I repeated it to myself all the way here. Now that I've told you, I don't have to remember all the words exactly."

He flies up and perches on my shoulder, then tickles my left ear with his beak. "That's bird language, to say I like you." He flies off before I can answer, through the window and off into the wide world. I watch him for as long as I can.

Actually, I hadn't really noticed the flowering cherry tree before. I'd always looked through its bare branches to what lay beyond. Now I realize what a sturdy tree it is. The part of the trunk I can see is straight. I can see only the right part of the top, since the left side is hidden by the wall. Looking closely, I can see dark brown buds sprouting all over the branches. So even though the tree looked bare all winter, it was really preparing new buds for spring. Strange. Invisible at first, but when you really look, you can see.

I've had six courses of chemotherapy over the past few months. Now the doctors are deciding what to do next. I hope I won't get more.

I feel as though I've been in the hospital forever. But everything happened so quickly at first. One day last fall, when I was playing soccer after school,

I slipped and fell down. It hurt, but I didn't think much about it. When the pain didn't stop after a few days, the doctor took x-rays, then blood tests. Soon I was admitted here to the hospital.

I was able to go home sometimes between courses of chemotherapy, and once I even went back to school for a few days. The chemotherapy was so strong that I lost my hair, so I wore a cap to cover my bald head. Although the other kids teased me about it at first, they soon got used to it and stopped.

This afternoon I saw my friend Lucy's mother in the doorway, holding a little baby in her arms. She stepped in from the corridor when she saw me looking at her.

"Hello again, Daniel," she said. "Here's little Alex. He's sweet, isn't he?"

She stroked the baby's head very gently. Alex opened his sleepy eyes.

"May I hold him for a minute?" I asked. Lucy's mother carefully put Alex into my arms. He was soft and warm and he kicked a little against my stomach for a second: I felt it, but I didn't say anything. Babies are beautiful.

Alex is only a month old. His sister, my friend Lucy, is my age—she's been here for two months or so. Her parents came together to see her for the first several weeks. Her mother looked very pregnant.

Then for a while Lucy's father came by himself, though her mother called a lot. Now all three of them come to see her. Lucy told me about Alex right after he was born.

Mom's sitting next to my bed, knitting. The clicking of the needles makes me sleepy, but I think about Alex and about being born. It's like what happens to a bud on the flowering cherry tree, really—when the time comes, the bud opens and the blossom appears.

I ask Mom, "What was it like for you when I was born? Did it hurt?"

She looks at me for a moment, then says, "Yes, it did hurt some, but I was so happy to see you that I forgot the pain right away."

That reminds me of what Victor said. "I guess that being born and dying are almost the same," I tell her. "They're both hard, but what comes next is so wonderful that you forget the hurt right away."

"I suppose you do," Mom says. Her voice sounds odd, the way it does when she's been crying. I hear the knitting needles start clicking once more.

My teacher, Mr. Simms, is here to see me. He sits to the left of my bed, next to the I.V. stand, with the bags of I.V. medicine dangling over his head. He doesn't seem to mind. I like it when he comes. He knows how to tell you things, especially things from history, but he tells them like interesting stories. When he talks about people in history, they seem real and alive.

Because I've missed so much school so far, I guess I'll have to repeat the year when I get back. In just a few months school will be out for the summer, and I first came to the hospital only a few months after class started. The principal came to see me soon after I got here, which was really nice of him because he had an hour's drive from his house and back. Still, I was relieved when he left. I don't really know him and I didn't know what to say. At least he didn't make a fuss. That can be awful. I know, because Aunt Ellie came to see me a while ago. She sat by my bed and all she could say was, "Oh, Daniel, it's so awful that you have to be lying there," and things like that. She sniffled and dabbed her eyes with her handkerchief. I don't want her to come again. Mom says she was like that because she's known a lot of grief. Well, she'd better cry about that to someone else, not me.

Mr. Simms puts a folder next to me on the bed. It's filled with drawings that the kids in class have made for me. Each one is signed, and I know all the names: Matthew, Keisha, Jason, Al, Suzanne . . . . I like Suzanne's drawing best. It's a large butterfly with a black body and gold wings with

blue on them. The butterfly is flying toward the sun and someone's waving good-bye to it.

"This one's my favorite."

"Do you want me to hang it up?" Mr. Simms asks.

"Yes, instead of that old picture. It looks too sad."

"Sad?" Mom asks, sounding surprised. "It always looked funny to me. But I can see that the butterfly will look wonderful there."

Mr. Simms takes the Donald Duck picture down from the wall. I get some tape from the bedstand drawer and give it to him to put up the butterfly. The room looks different now.

Today I'm more comfortable. I'm sitting up in bed, propped up on the pillows. I played Monopoly with Mom this morning. The game lasted a long time.

Victor came again yesterday, while Mom was getting lunch. He always comes when she's out of the room. That's fine with me. He said that he had something very difficult to tell me, something that he had trouble remembering. The golden bird had made him repeat it three times before he came to me.

"You see," he said, "when you look at the flowering cherry in winter, it looks dead. But it isn't—

it's dormant, which means that its growth is waiting for spring. It's alive, even if you can't see that. It'll be easy to see in a couple of days."

"I can see it now if I look carefully. It's as if the tree's moving."

"So it is," said Victor. "Anyway, where was I? Oh, yes. When the cherry tree looks alive, in full bloom, it's hard to imagine that it will look dead in autumn when the leaves fall. But it's the same tree, in fall or spring, whether going dormant or coming into bloom. You don't think of that in the spring, but it's true. The blossoming tree has some dormancy in it, and the dormant tree has some blossoming in it. But now I have to get some water, because the difficult part comes next."

Victor flew to the bedstand and took three sips of water from the glass. He came back to the railing at the foot of the bed, moved his beak as if searching for words, then went on: "It's like two sides of the same coin. What looks dead is alive, and what looks alive is already dying a little. Difficult, isn't it? But the golden bird said you'd understand some of it."

Victor scratched himself slowly and thoroughly with one leg, happy to have succeeded in telling his message.

"I'm glad if you can understand it, Daniel, because it's all very difficult for me. But then, I'm a bird, and you're a human being."

"I can't say I understand it completely myself. But I do feel that it's true. Even though Dad's body is dead, I feel that his spirit is alive somewhere else. I've seen him. I think that's what the golden bird means."

"Well, I'll go back and say so," Victor says. He flies to my shoulder, tickles my ear, and then he is gone.

I'm looking at a book that Mom brought from Gran today. Gran hardly ever comes herself, since she can't get around very easily these days. But she calls me twice a week, on Mondays and Thursdays at exactly seven o'clock.

Gran told me about the book last week. "It's filled with photographs of paintings," she said. "Maybe you're a little young for it, but your father liked paintings so much."

I like some of the paintings more than others. I look at one called "Jacob's Ladder" again and again. There's a ladder, like a long wooden painter's ladder, reaching from the earth to the sky. Someone's climbing on it and has gotten more than halfway up. There's a big gateway in the sky at the top of the ladder. A figure is standing in the gateway, glowing like the sun, with arms outstretched as if waiting for the climber. There are fields beyond the gateway, like the fields where I saw Dad, all green and bright. Is the figure in the gateway God?

Helen, the nurse, is here again today. I'm glad. She had two days off, but now she's back and she came to see me right away. Helen likes paintings. She's been to a museum where they had lots of paintings by artists from all over the world. When I'm better and they can let me out for a few days, she's going to take me there.

Helen's brought me a book with paintings by Vincent van Gogh. There are lots of blossoming trees. In a few more days the cherry tree will look just like them. It's like having a van Gogh painting outside my window.

I showed Helen the ladder painting from Gran's book. She liked the colors a lot—they're greens and blues, but the sort of greens and blues you see in dreams, not outside. The ladder painting is about three hundred years old, Helen says, and it was the artist's last work. Helen thinks that the figure in the gateway is God too.

I asked her to cut two small branches from the cherry tree so that I can watch the buds grow and open right in my room. She said she really shouldn't, but that she'd make an exception since I've had to be inside for so long.

I wonder about that, about having to be here, and having to go through chemotherapy and everything. Why me? My friend Suzanne has never been sick like this. It isn't fair. I don't mean that it isn't fair that Suzanne hasn't been sick—that's great for her—but why should some kids, like me and Josh, get so sick? I'll ask Helen whether she understands. I can ask Helen anything. I don't want to ask Mom, because her voice gets all funny.

Did I do something wrong to make me get sick? What was it? I know that I was angry and upset when Dad died. Maybe that's why?

Dr. Grant is coming through the door. We call him Dr. John. Now he's at the end of my bed where my charts and papers hang. He picks them up and reads them without looking at me. Mom says nothing and goes on knitting. Dr. John often laughs and cracks jokes. Not today. He's frowning. He puts the papers back and says, "We'd like to wait awhile to see what the test results are, to see how well the last course of treatment worked, Daniel. I think that's best."

I'm glad. No more treatment. At the same time, I feel cold inside.

"I'll give you some other medicine for the pain, through the I.V. Is the I.V. still all right? It's in your foot, isn't it? Let's have a look."

I pull back the sheet and Dr. John carefully feels my foot. "No pain there?" he asks.

"No."

"Good. In that case we'll leave it where it is for now." He pulls up the sheet, rests his hand briefly on Mom's shoulder, and says, "Take care, you two."

At the doorway, he turns. "Let me know if it hurts, okay? We have different medicines for pain, if you need them. I'll be back tomorrow to see you." He closes the door. He must be very busy, since he didn't stay long today. I hear his footsteps go down the corridor, then fade away.

Mom puts down her knitting. "Would you like something to drink, Daniel?"

"Some water, please,"

Mom takes a glass and rinses it under the tap before pouring in water from the jug and giving it back to me.

"Mom, will this go on much longer?"

Tears spring up in her eyes. "I don't know, honey."

I hate it when she's sad, but I don't know how to comfort her.

Lucy's mother stops in my room every day now, bringing Alex with her. Sometimes I ask to hold him, like the first day. He smiled last time, but Lucy told me later that when she got to hold him he started crying. I wish I had a younger brother or sister. It would be fun. And I think Mom would like it. Once I asked her and she said that it might've been nice to have a daughter too, but it was wonderful enough to have one child, especially if it was me. Not only wonderful, she said, but amazing, since the doctor had told her and Dad that they couldn't have children. I think that somehow I knew how much Mom wanted a baby, and since I wanted the most loving mother in the world, I came to her. So maybe it wasn't so amazing after all.

Today I got a postcard from Aunt Beth in New Zealand. "Get better quick," she writes, "because I want to meet you soon." She wrote to Mom, too, and sent some photographs. We looked at them together. The photos show the farm, my cousin Daniel and his two sisters, and sheep—Aunt Beth and her husband raise sheep. The sheep look fatter than any I've seen here. I really hope that I'll get better so that Mom and I can go and see them for ourselves.

Suddenly the green bird lands on the windowsill. This is the first time it has ever come back. Victor comes every day. Sometimes he comes and just tickles my ear, but other times he tells me things, like how it feels to fly, or how the golden bird's nest is doing. The first egg is already laid, Victor says, and it's all golden and sparkling in the sun.

The green bird sits very still on the windowsill, then flies to the cherry tree and perches on one of the branches. Now I can see: the first blossom is out, and it's so beautiful!

But the branches Helen brought in for me haven't bloomed yet. The tree beat them to it.

"Mom, look! The green bird's in the cherry tree and the first blossom is out."

Mom gets up and walks to the window. "Strange," she says. "That parrot must have escaped from somewhere. I hope it survives." The green bird flies upward, the gold flecks in its wings glistening and sparkling.

It's hurting again. Worse than usual. I feel like crying. I wish that I hadn't been mean to Mom when she put sugar in her tea this afternoon. She looked at me, but hardly said a word, just that she'd forgotten.

Now it's late, about three o'clock in the morning. I can't sleep. It hurts a lot. Winnie has given me more pain medicine, but it doesn't help enough.

I can hear rumbling noises coming from somewhere downstairs. The basement, I think. Maybe it's the boiler. Whatever it is, it's scary. I want to yell but I don't. I tell myself to lie still and try not to think of anything, but it doesn't work. I can't turn off my thoughts like the sound of a radio. I hear rustling and see shadows move on the wall, as if bats are flapping through the room. I wish Mom was here, but she's sleeping. She usually goes to the parents' rooms about nine o'clock, that's where she stays now. I won't ask them to wake up Mom. She's tired enough as it is.

I wish I was dead and with Daddy. I'm so tired. It's hard to fight against it all the time. I can barely fight anymore. My cheeks are wet from crying. Luckily it's dark and no one can see.

Suddenly there's a spot of light next to my bed. It gets bigger and bigger, until it becomes a figure glittering with light. It looks like God, the way God was painted in that picture of Jacob's Ladder, only much more beautiful. The pain disappears. I'm not scared and I'm not tired anymore. I'm happy. The figure leans toward me and puts a hand on my forehead, saying, "Don't forget that I am always with you, Daniel, even when you can't see me." I never knew that having a hand on my head could mean so much. Everything terrible fades away . . . then it's dark again. Before I know it, I fall asleep.

Mom's sitting next to me, knitting. I like the sound. My eyes are closed. No pain since last night. I can still see the figure of light before me. It was so beautiful. I've never been as happy as I was then.

"That's a happy smile, Daniel," Mom says suddenly.

I keep my eyes closed and say, "Someone came to see me last night. I think it was God. I'm not scared anymore." Mom doesn't speak, she just takes my hand. We're quiet for a long time. When I open my eyes I see tears running down Mom's face, but she's happy, too, I can tell from her expression. This time she doesn't wipe the tears away quickly. She kisses me and goes back to her knitting.

I close my eyes and see the figure of light again. I feel happy. Tired, too, but not in a bad way.

Victor's back on the end of my bed. Mom has gone to eat supper. He flaps his wings happily—he's never done that before.

"I heard that God was here last night," he says.

I nod, thinking about how it felt to have that hand on my forehead. "I hope it will happen again."

"It will, when the golden bird comes back for you."

Both of us are quiet for a minute. "Victor, I want to ask you something."

"Go ahead."

"I'm not going to get better, am I?"

"Not in the way you mean. But you'll be starting a new life soon. And now you have some idea how good that will be."

"So that's what the golden bird meant? It's like dying and being born."

"Yes, Daniel, that's right."

Victor flies to my pillow, tickles my ear, then leaves once more. I want to think about what he has said.

Suddenly I notice that the blossoms on the cherry tree are almost fully out. The buds have opened and the tree's covered with rosy flowers. I've never seen such a beautiful tree. Did it hurt the tree when the buds opened?

Mom's sitting next to me again. She's back from supper. She smiles and tells me she didn't put any sugar in her coffee.

Her knitting needles start clicking once more. She's moved on to the other sleeve now.

Suddenly I say, "Mom, I'm dying, aren't I?"

"Daniel!" she cries out, and then begins to sob. The tears pour down her cheeks. At last she says, "I'm afraid so, Daniel." She stands up and bends over the bed. We hug each other hard. We're both crying. "Oh Daniel, it hurts me so much," Mom says in a soft voice.

When we've stopped crying, Mom gets a tissue and wipes first her face, then mine, gently.

"Mom, what's awful is that I'll have to wait so long to see you again."

"You know," she says, "time passes differently in heaven. I'll be there before you know it."

I think Mom's right. I'll have to check with Victor. So it will only be a little while before all three of us—Mom, Dad, and me—are back together again. It will seem much longer to Mom, though. How sad for her to have to be here alone without us.

Helen's on night shift. That means that she'll be here until half past eleven. I'm glad, because I want to talk with her. I've asked her to come and see me when she has a chance. She's usually busy earlier in the evening, but things start settling down at about nine, when the smaller kids are asleep or at least tucked in for the night.

My friend Lucy just came to see me. She's able to be up and around again. She's had two courses of chemotherapy, and she'll be getting another one next week. She's lost most of her hair, which upsets her. Lucy had lovely long hair. I didn't mind it that much when my own hair went. It'll grow again, after a while. It has already started to grow back a little.

Lucy didn't stay too long, because I get tired quickly. She brought me something—it's in an envelope that has a blossom from the cherry tree taped to it. Lucy knows how much I like the blossom. Inside the envelope is a photograph of little Alex.

His eyes are open and he's laughing. Lucy said that her mother gave her the photograph and she thought I should have one too. I've put it on the bedstand against the vase with the cherry branches. Seven buds opened last night. If I touch the petals very gently, they feel silky. They're so soft, as soft as Alex is.

Now Helen comes in.

"Would you like something to drink, Daniel?"

"Maybe some juice?" I like it because it's cold. Helen goes off to get some. When she comes back, I show her the photograph of Alex.

"Do you want children, Helen?" I ask her.

"I do, but all in good time. I'll want one of them to look like you."

"Aren't you scared of the pain when they're born?"

"Not really, no. It doesn't last long, and you forget it afterward."

"Helen, it's so awful that Mom has to stay behind on her own. I'm all she's got."

Helen leans over and takes both my hands in one of hers. She sits on the side of the bed and strokes my face.

"You're right, it is awful, Daniel. But there are a lot of people who love her and they'll take care of her."

I snuggle close to Helen and then burst into tears. "It's so unfair! I've only lived for a few years. What have I done wrong?"

Helen strokes my head very gently. I feel safer now.

"You haven't done anything wrong, Daniel." I feel her cheek against my head. Then I hear her say softly, "I think it's unfair too. I don't understand it any more than you do." I can tell that she's crying too.

We sit close together for a long time. I feel calmer but also very tired. "I don't want to talk about it anymore," I tell her.

"There's no reason why you should. But let me know when you're afraid, or if you feel pain." Helen lays me gently back against the pillows, then pulls the blanket up and smoothes it out. I'm so tired.

"You promise to let me know?" she asks.

"I promise."

"I'll stay here now until you fall asleep," Helen says. She sits down again and holds my hand. I fall asleep right away and don't wake up once the whole night.

It's light out when I open my eyes. The cherry tree is in full bloom now. I look at it and think of Vincent van Gogh. Helen told me that he painted his most beautiful paintings when he was very sad. Although I don't make beautiful paintings, I do see

the most beautiful things when I'm tired—lately I feel as though I'm seeing things for the first time. The cherry tree is so beautiful, it almost hurts to look at it. Tears come down my face. I brush them away quickly, because Mom will be here soon and I don't want her to see me crying.

Suddenly I remember what I dreamed last night. I was trying to get down corridors and tunnels, some of them so narrow I could barely squeeze through. Then I came to a small hallway that was lit with a sort of neon light. On the other side of the hall was a dark narrow tunnel that climbed steeply upward. I had to get through that tunnel, but first, in order to get in, I had to climb a big barrier right in the middle of the hall. Luckily I managed to find a hole in the barrier and get through to the tunnel. I took one step in. How steep it was! I felt so tired all of a sudden. Would all these passageways go on forever? Then, in a flash, I could see that the end of the tunnel opened out onto a plain full of beautiful colors, where the sun was shining, bright and warm. For a moment I realized with delight that it would be wonderful there. Then a voice—I don't know from where—told me that this was heaven. I felt stronger. Then I was back in the tunnel for an instant, and the dream ended.

The cherry tree reminds me of that plain in my dream, it's so beautiful. All the buds on the branches in the vase on my bedstand are open now too. It's all in flower.

It must be fun to be a gardener and see flowers open and bloom, year after year. I used to want to be a pilot, then later, a train engineer like Dad was, sitting in the front of the train, watching everything race by. I wanted to ride on one of those superfast special trains that travel hundreds of miles per hour. Dad would have liked being the engineer on one of those.

My friend John sent me a photograph of a train like that. He's in my class. He went on a trip with his parents and bought the postcard especially for me. The card is tacked to the wall by my bed, along with all the others from friends and family. There must be eighty cards up there. I've saved most of my cards in a box, but the best ones are up on the wall.

One of Gran's postcards shows a big shaggy sheepdog, my favorite kind. We used to have one at home, named Tom—he'd been my parents' dog before I was born. He played with me a lot when I was little, even though he was old by then. He lived a long time. Then finally, one night, he died in his sleep. We dug a hole in the garden and buried him on top of his blanket, then put another blanket over him. I gathered some stones and piled them up to mark his grave. I found a big flat stone and painted his name in gold letters on it, then placed the flat stone in front of the others. The stone got mossy after a while, but I didn't clean it—I liked it that way. I'd like to get another dog sometime, but not exactly the same kind. Maybe a female, so that we could have puppies.

I wonder how the golden bird's nest is coming along. I don't suppose that it will be too long now before I can see it. I wonder how many young birds there will be: probably about seven, I guess.

Mom comes in. I tell her to look out the window. She steps over to it, then smiles. "The cherry tree is splendid, Daniel. I think it's flowering just for you."

"Why does it blossom for such a short time, Mom? It only lasts a few days, especially when the days are windy. It isn't fair that something so beautiful lasts only a little while."

Mom turns from the window to me, with tears in her eyes. Her lips move but no words come out. Finally she says, "That's something I don't understand, Daniel. But let's enjoy the blossoms' beauty while it lasts." She goes to the bedstand, picks up the vase with its blooming branches, and takes it to the sink. "I'll give them some more water. They need a lot of water when they're in flower."

More pain tonight, not just in my stomach but in my whole body. Winnie is the nurse on this shift. I told her that it hurt and she called the doctor. Now she's given me more pain medicine. She puts a light on in my room and sits beside me. She has left the door open to the hall, so that she can hear if any of the other kids call out. She's holding my hand. Every so often I press her hand as hard as I can, and she presses back gently. I can't sleep.

The room gets misty. I can see only the outlines of things. The butterfly on the wall has lost its color. Then the television set starts to glow, though the image is hazy, without color, and it looks as though it's snowing on the screen. The mist's getting thicker, so thick that I can't distinguish anything anymore.

Now the pain's starting to go away. The room's getting darker, even though a light is on.

Winnie stands up and tells me, "I'll be back soon, Daniel." I lie alone in the dark. I close my eyes and try to breathe calmly and regularly. It isn't easy. Suddenly I feel someone holding my hand. I open my eyes. "Daddy!" My father is slowly stroking my chest with his other hand. "You can go to sleep now, Daniel. Don't be frightened, nothing can harm you anymore." The pain goes away completely. I haven't felt this well in a long time.

"Will you stay with me?" I ask him.

"Yes, Daniel. In a moment you'll stop seeing me, but I'll still be here beside you. Soon I'll be going with you to the golden bird's nest."

He is wearing the same clothes he wore in my dream, a white suit and a blue shirt. Light seems to be streaming from him. He's standing beside my bed, holding my hand tightly.

"There, that feels better, doesn't it?" What a wonderful face Dad has.

Now Winnie comes back and sits down by my bed. She walks right through Dad. Strange. Everything in the room has come back to normal. The mist has gone and the light is on.

"How's the pain, Daniel?" she says.

"It's all gone. Dad took it away. It just disappeared."

Winnie takes my hand.

"That's good. So the pain medicine must be working. You'll soon fall asleep now. Do you want me to tuck you in? I'll turn off the light and leave the door open. Just let me know if you want anything."

I feel as though I'm drifting. When I wake up, everything seems different. I can see the television and the bedstand, and yet I can't. It's as if I'm looking through them, as if they're weightless, drifting in space. Nothing has any weight anymore: I could lift the television set with one finger. People's voices seem to come from far away, as if they can hardly reach me. It's like a movie I once saw about mountaineering, where three people were climbing up a steep mountain. They were roped together. You could see the mountaintop above them, and above that the wide open sky. Beautiful. Their voices sounded different too, somehow, maybe because the air was so clear and there was nothing in the way.

I can't see Dad. Mom is sitting next to me now, but even she seems to be far away. It's strange that Dad feels so much closer.

"Would you like some water, Daniel?" Mom asks.

Her voice disturbs the silence of the room. I'd rather stay in the quiet. I'm not sure why. But it's so peaceful when I'm drifting like this and everything seems weightless.

I shake my head, then say, "I don't want to talk right now."

Mom is quiet for a moment. I hear the knitting needles quickly clicking, though they sound farther away than usual too. Then she says, "That's all right, Daniel. I'm here if you need me."

Helen comes in. "More mail for you, Daniel. Lots of cards."

Though I hear what Helen says, I keep seeing those mountains and the wide sky above, and I watch the mountaineers climb higher and higher, one after the other. I keep my eyes closed. If I open them, the weightless world may vanish.

"Thank you, Helen," Mom says. "Daniel's tired today. I think he just wants to sleep."

I hear Helen's footsteps come closer, then they go away again.

The first mountaineer has nearly reached the top. There's sweat on his forehead, but his hands and feet move very calmly, as if he has just begun the climb. Watching him, I fall asleep.

Victor's here. He lands on the windowsill outside, like the first time. His blue feathers look beautiful against the rosy blossoms of the tree. I'm happy that he's here—he and the cherry tree belong to the world of the mountaineers, just as Dad does.

Victor flies through the window to perch on the foot of my bed.

"Here I am again, Daniel."

I smile, the way I always do when I see him.

"This is the last time I'll visit you here. The golden bird will be coming back for you tomorrow."

"That's good. Victor, I want to be up there so much, up at the top of the world."

"You're nearly there, Daniel. You know, the very last part isn't difficult. You feel the great space around you at the top of the mountain, and the ordinary world lies far below you, so far below that it hardly hurts anymore to leave it behind for good."

Victor ruffles his feathers, then stretches his neck back and pecks at them. It's what he usually does when he has something difficult to say.

"Oh, Daniel, I guess I don't need to explain much more. The golden bird said that you'd understand."

"It's true . . . I think I do. I understand it with my head and I feel it inside."

He flies to my shoulder as usual and tickles my ear. "So I'll see you tomorrow, at the golden bird's nest. We'll be waiting for you, Daniel."

"How many baby birds are in the nest?" I ask him.

"Seven. The last egg hatched today. They look so beautiful."

Victor flies in the air and right through the window as he speaks. I watch him until he's just a dot in the distance. When he's gone, I look at my hand. I know it's mine—I recognize the nails, the shape, the marks from the I.V. And yet it doesn't belong to me. It belongs to the world below, in the valley, not to the world at the top of the mountain. How strange to see things so differently.

Mom's sitting beside me again, knitting. The clicking of the needles is the only sound in the room. My eyes are closed, and I'm still watching the first mountaineer as he slowly approaches the top. The sun is shining on the highest slopes, though the climber is still in the shade. The other two are only a short distance behind him, and all three of them are still linked with ropes.

The sound of knitting stops, and I feel Mom's hand on mine. But it hurts to be touched now. I can see the top mountaineer look down. He seems unsure for a second, then turns his head and at last regains his balance.

"Please don't," I say to Mom, and move my hand

away. I keep my eyes closed. Although I don't look at Mom, I know there are tears on her cheeks.

The mountaineers are still climbing in the shade. Light streams down from the top of the peak. Just a little farther and the first climber will reach the light.

I'm tired now, very tired. I can't even speak. I fall asleep in the quiet room.

When I wake up, Mom is knitting again.

"Gran called," she tells me. "She asked me to give you three big kisses."

I think of Gran as Mom gets up and kisses me gently three times. I keep my eyes closed. Mom holds her cheek against mine for a while without speaking. Her cheek is wet. Then she sits down next to my bed again.

"Mom, please give Bear to Gran soon."

Bear is the teddy bear that Gran gave me when I was born, so he's as old as I am. He's been everywhere with me. In the hospital he has always been at the foot of my bed. Before Victor came, Bear looked sad sometimes and I'd give him a hug. It was easy to tell when he was sad because he'd sit sort of lopsided, with his head hanging down a little. Bear knows everything about me. I know that Gran will take care of him.

I see the climbers again. The one in front is nearest to the top. He has reached the light now, and the middle one is almost there. The third one, the last one, seems to be climbing more slowly. I can see them calling to one another. The first two climbers stop, while the last one climbs on up toward the light. Then I listen. The climbers seem to be singing.

The music is faint but clear, though it's hard to hear the words.

"They're nearly there," I tell Mom. "They're singing now." She takes my hand again.

The words are about coming into the light, about God's hand reaching down to those who climb up the mountain. I hear the last words clearly, "No shadows now, no pain, in the full light of God's love." I repeat them out loud. "It's beautiful, Mom."

"Yes, it is, Daniel," she says softly. " 'No shadows now, no pain, in the full light of God's love . . .' "

The last climber has caught up and the other two can continue. They all climb on. I keep my eyes on the top one. He's almost there. Suddenly I see the sun rising high behind the mountaintop. How beautiful the light is, how vast and intense. There's so much light that sparks seem to be flying off the top climber, and now the middle one too.

Dr. John comes in. I know without opening my

eyes that he's here, since his footsteps are heavier than Mom's or Helen's. I'm so tired that I can't keep my eyes open any longer. I hear him ask Mom, "How's he doing?" and hear Mom reply, "He's asleep most of the time now." I don't hear Dr. John leave. I think he's staying here with Mom for a while.

The climbers have arrived, all three of them. They're all at the top of the mountain. They're holding hands, and the sun is streaming out over their heads. They've made it! The middle one unfurls a blue and gold banner, then ties it to a pole. The banner waves in the breeze at the very top of the mountain.

"Daniel, it's time to go."

I open my eyes. It's Daddy. I sit up in bed.

"Look, Daniel. Look at the window. The golden bird's on the way."

I look at the window. The cherry blossoms are beautiful. Suddenly, the golden bird flies through the blossoms to the windowsill and looks at me again through bright, pale eyes.

"Mom, there's the golden bird." I look to the right where she's sitting and I can see the outline of her face. "I'm going to the golden bird's nest, and Dad's going with me." I think that Mom is saying something, but I can't hear the words. I have

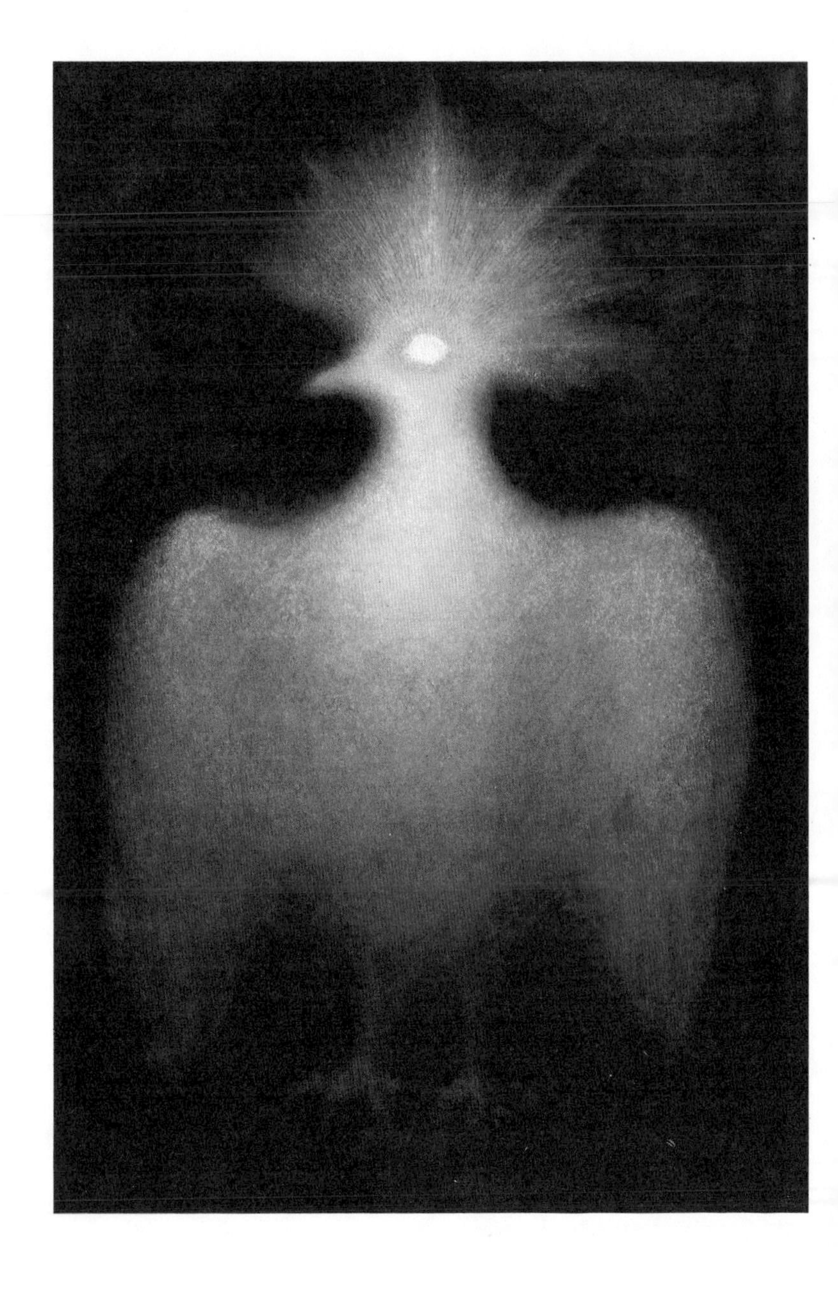

to look back at the golden bird's eyes. They're calling me to come. I float toward the golden bird and reach for Dad's hand.

"Come on, Daddy, we're going."

No more pain, no more tiredness. Just light and weightlessness. The golden bird flies toward the sun. We follow, floating upward, past the flowering cherry tree.

Hans Stolp

is a pastor who worked with hospitalized children for nine years. He is the author of several books for adults, but this is his first children's book. He lives in the Netherlands.

Lidia Postma

has illustrated many books for children, among them *The Twelve Dancing Princesses and Other Tales from Grimm* (Dial), *The Witch's Garden, Tom Thumb, The Stolen Mirror,* and *Hans Christian Andersen's Fairy Tales,* for which she received the Gold Brush Award. In 1979 Ms. Postma won the Golden Apple at the Biennale of Illustrations in Bratislava. She has two sons and lives on a houseboat in Amsterdam.